The Christmas Ship

The Christmas Ship

By Dean Morrissey

HarperCollins Publishers

Please visit Dean Morrissey's web site at
www.deanmorrisseybooks.com

The Christmas Ship
Copyright © 2000 by Dean Morrissey
Story and pictures by Dean Morrissey;
written by Dean Morrissey and Stephen Krensky
Printed in the U.S.A. All rights reserved. www.harperchildrens.com

Library of Congress Cataloging-in-Publication Data
Morrissey, Dean.
    The Christmas ship / by Dean Morrissey
        p.   cm.
    Summary: Joey and Sam the toymaker board a magical ship to help Father Christmas
distribute gifts on Christmas Eve.
    ISBN 0-06-028575-3. — ISBN 0-06-028576-1 (lib. bdg.) — ISBN 0-06-443605-5 (pbk.)
    [1. Toys—Fiction.   2. Christmas—Fiction.   3. Santa Claus—Fiction.   4. Magic—
Fiction.]   I. Title.
PZ7.M84532Ch   2000   99-27598
[Fic]—dc21   CIP
                                                                                                                              AC

Typography by Elynn Cohen
❖

For Shan and Ian

It was still early on Christmas Eve. The village toy maker, Sam Thatcher, was hard at work, hoping to finish up all the toys before dark.

Thump, thump!

All around him were hundreds of toys. They lined the shelves and spilled onto the floor.

THUMP!

What was that noise?

Sam went to the front door. Outside, his friends—Joey, Sarah, and Michael—were throwing snowballs.

"Careful," he warned them. "If you hit this old shop too hard, it might fall into the harbor and sink my boat."

Joey stopped in mid throw. "Could that really happen?" he asked. Sam's shop did look a bit rickety.

"Not the way you throw," said Sarah.

Michael started to laugh, but his face suddenly froze.

"See you later," he whispered, and darted round the corner.

Joey and Sarah turned around. Michael's father, the town mayor, was approaching.

"Merry Christmas, Mr. Mayor," Sam said.

The mayor waved the comment aside. "Never mind all that. You've had six months to make the repairs I ordered." He stepped into the shop. "It doesn't look like you've even started."

Sam sighed. "Mayor, I just need a little more time. I have every intention of—"

"You've had long enough!" snapped the mayor. "This shop is falling apart. I'm closing you down."

The mayor picked up a stone and nailed a sign to the door.

CONDEMNED
PER ORDER OF
THE MAYOR

Joey and Sarah followed Sam back into the shop.

"There must be something we can do," said Joey.

"Yes," said Sam, "there is. Go home and get ready for Christmas. But not without these. . . ."

He picked up two presents and gave them out.

"It's beautiful!" said Sarah, peering into her telescope.

"Mine, too," said Joey, examining his sailboat. "But what about the shop?"

"Don't worry about that," Sam told them. "Now hurry on home. It's getting late."

Once the children were out of sight, Sam sat down wearily. The shop—condemned! He knew he should start packing up, but he couldn't bring himself to begin. He just sat under the rising moon, not even bothering to light a fire.

Suddenly he heard a clattering on the roof. A gust of wind stirred the ashes in his fireplace and rushed through the room, knocking some toys off the shelves. Then, with a great *whoosh*, a visitor came right down the chimney.

"Father Christmas!" exclaimed Sam. They were old friends, and sometimes Sam filled special orders that came from the North Pole. "Need some last-minute stocking stuffers?"

Father Christmas shook his head. "Not tonight, Sam. Actually, there's a big storm brewing over the ocean, and I'm running behind. I need you to make my deliveries here in Old Bridgeport."

"Me?" said Sam. "But how? I have no sleigh, no reindeer." *And soon no shop,* he added to himself.

Father Christmas smiled. "True enough," he said. "But I know you'll find a way."

And without another word, he was gone.

Sam shook his head. "How can I possibly deliver so many presents?"

He bent down to pick up the fallen toys.

"To do that, I'd need some sort of . . ."

The stuffed rabbit at his fingertips suddenly sat up.

". . . magic." Sam looked around the room. All the fallen toys were standing and stretching and walking around.

Sam laughed out loud. "Well, Father Christmas, I see you've taken care of my helpers. But what about the sleigh?"

The rabbit hopped to the window and pressed
its nose against the glass.

Sam went over for a look.

There was his boat, tied up to the dock. But
even in the dark Sam could tell something was different.

He hurried outside, and the toys shuffled along beside him.

Father Christmas had been busy.

On either side of the boat the fishing nets lay heavy with
brightly wrapped gifts. And a scroll of names hung from the
ship's wheel.

"Quiet!" Sam whispered, as the toys scampered on board.
"Everyone is asleep."

But Sam was mistaken. In his attic bedroom just a few houses
away, Joey tossed and turned, worrying about Sam and his shop.

Suddenly Joey heard a noise outside. He looked out the window
to see Sam walking toward his boat. But who was with him? Why,
they looked almost like . . .

"Toys!" he cried, jumping up and throwing his coat right over
his pajamas.

On board the ship the toys climbed up the rigging and unfurled the sails.

"Here now," said Sam, "be careful!"

The toys scampered from stem to stern, casting off lines. As the ship came free of the dock, Sam ran for the wheel. A sudden wind filled the sails.

"Hang on, everyone!" said Sam, not sure himself what would happen next.

At that moment the bow rose from the water, and the little ship sailed into the sky.

As Sam worked to steer the boat, it lunged to starboard—and Joey tumbled out of the hatch.

"Hello, Sam!" he said.

"Joey, what are you doing here?"

There was a long pause as Joey looked back down to the harbor. "I'm not sure."

"Never mind," said Sam. He told Joey what was happening. "There's no time to return you home now, so make yourself useful. Go to the bow and keep a good lookout."

"Aye, aye, sir!"

With Joey shouting instructions and Sam consulting the list, the ship sailed on. At each house the toys lowered rope ladders over the rail and gathered up the presents.

It took practice . . .

and more practice . . .

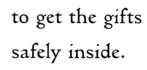

to get the gifts
safely inside.

Five houses, then ten, and soon Joey lost count. But he noticed when they arrived at the mayor's house.

"I'll take down Michael's gift," Joey offered.

"What about his father's?" asked Sam.

Joey frowned. "Do we have any coal on board?"

Sam pointed at his list. "Joey, the mayor's name is right here." He reached into the net. "And here's his gift. So let's show a bit more Christmas spirit, eh?"

Joey just sighed.

Silently they entered the house. Joey put Michael's gift in his stocking while
Sam placed the mayor's on the mantel. Then they quickly went out again.

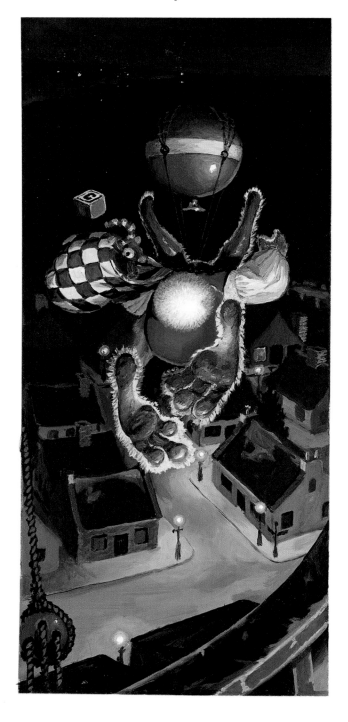

street by street,

Long into the night, Sam and his crew sailed over the village. They made their way through Father Christmas' list and room by room.

house by house,

The stars were winking out when Sam and Joey finally finished. As the ship neared the harbor, it slowly descended, like a balloon losing air. The toys secured the last lines, but they began to yawn and stumble about.

"I think the magic is winding down," said Sam.

When the ship docked, he and Joey carried the slumbering toys back inside.

"Well, we did it," said Sam.

"I know, I know! The toys were great—and wait till Michael finds out I delivered his present! And Sarah, she'll . . ."

Joey frowned. "But what about the shop, Sam?"

"Never mind about that now. It's almost morning." Sam patted Joey's shoulder. "Now you run on home."

The harbor was now quiet and empty.

Sam watched as
Joey returned to his
house. Someone else
was watching, too.
It was the mayor.
He stared hard at
the shop door. Then
he took out his new
hammer and pulled
down his sign.

"Merry Christmas!" he muttered, his face softening briefly before his scowl returned.

But it was too late. The wind had picked up the kindness in his words,
and carried them across the village and into the early morning.

And once a spirit like that gets out . . .

. . . almost anything can happen.